# Samira
# the Superhero
# Fairy

by Daisy Meadows

ORCHARD

www.rainbowmagic.co.uk

# Jack Frost's Spell

It sounds like fun to wear a cape,
And always make a quick escape.
And with a superpower or two,
What shocking damage I could do!

Frostman will be Samira's doom.
I'll take her things! Kapow! Kaboom!
Those super-zero fools will flee.
The only hero will be ME!

# The
# Crimson Cape

# Contents

# Paws in Peril

"I love absolutely everything about summer," said Kirsty Tate, who was skipping down Tippington High Street with her best friend Rachel Walker. "I love the sunshine and the long days — and most of all I love you staying with me for a whole week. We're going to have so much fun."

"I can't stop smiling," said Rachel. "I'm so excited about this film."

The girls were on their way to Tippington's little cinema. It was showing the brand-new summer blockbuster *Dragon Girl and Tigerella*, starring the girls' favourite superheroes.

"I can't wait to find out what adventures Dragon Girl and Tigerella are going to have," said Kirsty. "It's going to be amazing to see them in a film together – that's never happened before."

"What do you like best about them?" asked Rachel.

"I like the way Dragon Girl flies through the sky so fast when she's going to save someone," said Kirsty. "It reminds me of our fairy friends when they want to help human beings."

"I love seeing Tigerella use her super strength," said Rachel. "Do you remember when she lifted a whole bus of schoolchildren with just one hand? She's so cool."

"The best part is that they have normal lives too, just like us," said Kirsty. "It's only when danger strikes that they become superheroes and go to help people. I wish I had a secret identity."

Rachel squeezed her best friend's hand.

"You do, in a way," she said. "After all, no one else knows that we are friends of Fairyland."

Just then, they heard a faint mew.

"That sounded like a cat," said Kirsty, looking around.

They were standing beside a high garden fence with a cherry tree inside. As Kirsty looked at the tree, she saw a ball of black fluff clinging to one of the branches. A pair of scared eyes peered at her through the petals.

"It's a kitten," she said. "I think it's stuck. We should go and tell the people who live here."

The kitten gave another sad mew and Rachel tried to open the garden gate.

"It's locked,"
she said.
"They must be
out. What are
we going to
do? We can't
just leave the
poor kitten
here."

She looked
up and down

the high street, hoping to see a grown-up to ask for help. But it was a quiet day in Tippington, and there was no one in sight.

"I wish we could call Dragon Girl or Tigerella in real life," said Kirsty. "Superheroes are always getting kittens out of trees."

She thought that Rachel would smile at this idea, but she didn't seem to be listening. Her mouth had fallen open and she was staring at the tree in delight. A streak of purple and gold was whizzing around the kitten, crackling with golden sparkles.

"It's magic," said Kirsty, smiling.

Whenever she and Rachel were together, magical adventures seemed to know exactly where to find the two

of them. The purple-and-gold light lifted
the kitten down from the tree and placed
it gently on top of the fence. It scampered
off at once, but the light stayed on the
fence. The glow faded a little, and the
girls saw that it was a tiny fairy. She was
wearing a purple-and-gold top with a

star on the front, starry
purple leggings and
long purple boots.
Red bracelets
circled both her
wrists, and her black
hair was tied back in
a plait.

"Greetings, friends
of Fairyland," she
said. "I'm Samira the
Superhero Fairy."

# Victory for a Villain

"It's wonderful to meet you, Samira," said Kirsty. "What are you doing here in Tippington?"

Samira flashed a beautiful smile.

"I heard your wish for a superhero," she said. "As Fairyland's resident superhero, I came flying to the rescue!"

"Thank you for helping the kitten," said Rachel.

"You're welcome," said Samira with a wink. "It's all in a day's work, but now I must fly. I hope we meet again!"

She started to spin around.

"Wait a moment," Rachel called out.

Samira stopped spinning and smiled questioningly.

"We're on our way to the cinema to see *Dragon Girl and Tigerella*," Rachel said. "Would you like to come and see it with us?"

"What a wonderful idea," said Samira. "I'd love to come."

"This day just keeps getting better," said Kirsty.

Rachel held open her T-shirt pocket and Samira dived inside. Then the girls

ran the rest of the way to the cinema,
feeling more excited than ever. Soon they
were cradled in red plush seats, clutching
boxes of warm popcorn and bottles
of fizzy water. Rachel put a few puffs
of popcorn into her T-shirt pocket for
Samira, and the film began.

At first, it was even better than they could have imagined. Dragon Girl had a thrilling chase through narrow city streets, and Tigerella had to leap across a burning bridge to save her brother from the arch-villain, The Mole. The girls gasped at the action scenes and giggled at The Mole, whose plans were always going wrong.

"The baddie gets all the funniest moments," said Kirsty, as they watched The Mole scurry into his underground tunnels.

But then something strange happened. Dragon Girl bumped into a lamppost, fell out of the sky and landed in a puddle with a loud splash. The audience laughed as she crawled out of the pond, bedraggled and muddy. Her dragon fire had been completely put out. Before she could stand, The Mole popped out of a nearby drain and dragged her into his underground tunnels. Dragon Girl tried to fly out of The Mole's grasp, but her powers didn't work.

A boy in the row in front turned to his friend with a frown.

"This isn't right," he whispered. "I've

read all the Dragon
Girl comics, and this has
never happened."

"He's right," said
Samira in a low voice.
"Oh my stars and spell
books, if superheroes
are losing their power
here in the human world,
there must be something wrong with my
magical objects in Fairyland. Will you
come to Fairyland to help me find out
what is going on?"

"Of course," said the girls.

They quickly slipped under their seats.
There was no one sitting beside them,
and everyone in the cinema had their
eyes fixed on the screen. Samira popped
out of Rachel's pocket and waved her

wand. They heard the sound of a loud, rushing wind and then suddenly they were whirling around so fast that it made them dizzy. When they could see again, they were flying across a bright-blue sky.

"We're fairies again," said Kirsty, fluttering her gauzy wings in delight.

"And we're in Fairyland," Rachel added, looking down.

The green hills of Fairyland stretched out beneath them. In one direction they could see the pink turrets of the Fairyland Palace. The opposite way, grey clouds hovered over Jack Frost's Ice Castle. They could see forests and glades dotted among toadstool cottages, sparkling streams, orchards and crystal pools.

"Look," said Samira, pointing straight ahead. "That's my home."

They were flying towards the tallest building that the girls had ever seen in Fairyland. It was a tall, thin tower made of gleaming metal, with a single spire at the top. It was so high that the fluffy white clouds were touching it.

"Welcome to the Silver Skyscraper," said Samira.

# An Awesome Apartment

As the fairies flew closer to the Silver Skyscraper, they saw that there was a small, round platform at the top of the spire.

"It's just big enough for the three of us to land on," said Samira. "But we'll have to be very close together."

They linked arms and fluttered down.

As soon as the tips of their toes touched the cold metal platform, a bubble of clear glass rose up around them.

"This is very cool," said Kirsty.

"You're now in the entry pod," said Samira. "Hold on to your wings – it gets even cooler."

The pod shot downwards into the hollow spire, so fast that their hair was blown upwards.

"It's like the best fairground ride ever!" Rachel said, squealing as they plunged down. Then the pod slowed, the glass lowered, and they were popped out like corks into a huge apartment.

"Is this where you live?" asked Kirsty in amazement.

"Yes," said Samira with a smile. "Do you like it?"

"It's amazing!" said Rachel.

They were standing on a white, fluffy rug in the middle of a huge open space. At one end of the room was a gleaming white kitchen. In the middle were modern black couches around a low coffee table. Comics were neatly piled on top. But the best part was the windows, which went from floor to ceiling almost all the way around the room. Wispy clouds floated past as they watched.

"From here, I can keep an eye on all of Fairyland and make sure that the fairies are safe," said Samira.

"It's wonderful," said Kirsty, gazing at the Fairyland Palace in the distance. "It must be like living in the sky."

There was
only one wall
that was not
made of glass,
and Samira
walked towards
it. A portrait of
Queen Titania
and King
Oberon was
hanging there,
and Rachel
and Kirsty went
to look at it.

"That's funny," said Kirsty, peering at
the picture. "I've never seen the queen
wearing that ruby ring before."

"You have sharp eyes," said Samira,
smiling. "I'm impressed."

She pressed the ruby ring with her finger, and suddenly the whole wall swivelled around to reveal a secret chamber. The only things inside were three empty pedestals.

"Oh no," said Samira with a groan. "My magical objects have gone. I knew something must have gone wrong, but this is as bad as it could be."

Rachel and Kirsty hurried to put their arms around her.

"Is this why the film went wrong?" Rachel asked.

Samira nodded.

"I have three magical objects," she explained. "The first is the crimson cape, which helps superheroes in stories everywhere to be able to fly. Without the cape, they won't even be able to get a toe

off the ground."

"But that means that Dragon Girl will be trapped underground with The Mole until the crimson cape is back where it belongs," said Kirsty.

"Yes," said Samira. "Also, the baddies will be able to fly, just like a superhero. That's going to make them even more difficult to catch. If only I knew who it was. I'm used to having a villain to catch, but this is a mystery."

Rachel and Kirsty exchanged a knowing glance.

"I think we can guess who did this,"

said Rachel. "Jack Frost is always causing trouble, and this seems like exactly the sort of thing he'd do."

"The Ice Lord?" said Samira with a shiver. "Galloping goblins! I have never crossed paths with him before."

"We have defeated him and his naughty goblins lots of times," said Kirsty.

"I can't bear the thought of them having my three magical objects," said Samira.

"What are the other two?" Kirsty asked.

"The all-seeing eye mask and the lively lasso," said Samira. "The eye mask helps superheroes to know who needs help, and the lasso helps them to act with courage and confidence. Without them, comics, films and storybooks will be turned upside down. Villains will win and superheroes will be defeated. Oh, girls, I have to find the missing objects! Will you help me?"

"Count us in!" said Rachel.

# A Mysterious Monster

Samira hurried over to the window that faced Jack Frost's Ice Castle. She narrowed her eyes and stayed very still.

"Are you all right?" Rachel asked.

"I'm using my super-sight," said Samira. "Thrilling thunderbolts! The air around the castle is green with flying goblins."

"That proves it," said Rachel. "The crimson cape is there."

"We have to go and get it," said Kirsty. "Until you have it back, Dragon Girl will be stuck in the underground tunnels with The Mole, and no superheroes will be able to fly in any of their stories."

"You're as brave as superheroes," said Samira.

Rachel looked around.

"How do we get out?" she asked. "There's no door."

Samira beckoned them over to the window to stand beside her.

"Press your hands against the glass," she said.

Kirsty and Rachel placed their palms on the glass. For a moment it felt cool and hard. Then the glass seemed to ripple, like water when you throw a stone into it.

"My hands are going through the glass!" said Kirsty, snatching them back.

"Don't be scared," said Samira. "This is my way out."

She went first, pushing her way through the glass until she was fluttering in the air on the other side. Rachel and Kirsty followed her.

"That was what I think it must be like to walk through a waterfall," said Rachel.

A few moments later they were zooming towards Jack Frost's Ice Castle. As they got nearer, they saw goblins somersaulting and diving around the castle and the gardens. Every single one of them had a shiny green cape tied around his neck. The fairies watched as goblins bumped into walls, careered

around trees, crash-landed in bushes and smashed into frozen ponds.

"Wands and wishbones!" said Samira. "This is terrible. The goblins don't know how to use their powers – they're going to get hurt."

"They don't seem to mind," Kirsty pointed out. "They're all giggling."

She was right. Every single goblin was cackling and hooting as they tried out

their new powers. Even the goblins who
had crashed into the castle wall were
lying on the
ground, helpless
with laughter.

"I don't think
they're going to
try to stop us," said Samira. "Now is our
chance. We have to fly into the heart of
the castle and find my missing objects."

They flew forwards, dodging the
tumbling goblins, and landed side by side
on the roof. At once they heard a loud
snorting sound.

"It's a wild monster!" Samira exclaimed.
"This looks like a job for a superhero!"

Rachel and Kirsty leaned over the turrets
and peered down into the castle courtyard,
and they couldn't help but laugh.

"It's not a monster," said Kirsty. "It's a snorer."

Samira leaned over the turrets too. Jack Frost was lying across a throne in the middle of the courtyard, covered in a little red blanket. His snores were echoing around the stone walls.

"Do you think that's his comfort blanket?" Rachel asked. "It's very small."

"Speckled sprites, that's not a blanket," Samira cried. "That's the crimson cape!"

# Frostman

"We have to do this quietly and slowly," Rachel said. "We mustn't wake Jack Frost up."

"We'll work as a team," said Samira. "Together, we'll lift the cape without him noticing a thing."

Holding hands, they fluttered down and landed beside Jack Frost. His snores were deafening.

"I'm sure I can feel the ground shaking," Samira whispered.

She gently picked up the neck of the cape. Rachel and Kirsty each took a corner. Then they started to lift.

"Slowly, slowly," Kirsty whispered to herself.

The silky material of the cape was light, and Jack Frost didn't stir as it began to lift off his body.

Suddenly, they heard a noise overhead.

"Ouch! Help! I can't see!"

They looked up and saw a goblin with his cape tangled over his head. He hovered for a moment, and then dropped like a stone – straight into Jack Frost's lap. The cape was yanked out of the fairies' hands.

"YOWEEEEE!" shouted Jack Frost.

"Hurray, a soft landing!" said the goblin, pulling his cape off his head. "That was lucky."

"You brainless baboon!" Jack Frost bellowed. "You pathetic pest! You chinless chump! You—"

He stopped because he suddenly caught sight of the fairies. His lips curled into a snarl, and he shoved the goblin off his lap. Clutching the crimson cape, he rose to his feet.

"You'll never get it back," he hissed.

He ran out of the castle and into the gardens. The fairies chased him, trying not to bump into any low-flying goblins.

Jack Frost turned and held up the cape.

"Come and get it then, if you're so super," he sneered.

Samira rocketed towards him, but he whipped the cape out of her way at the

last second. He doubled over laughing as she turned and hovered, glaring at him with her arms folded.

"There's nothing super about you after all," he cackled.

He put the cape
around his neck
and swaggered
up and down.
"You can't stop me,"
he said. "I'm a superhero
now. I'm Frostman!
I can even fly, just like
you."

Suddenly an idea popped into Rachel's mind.

"He might be able to fly, but he's had no practice," she whispered to Samira and Kirsty. "We can't get the cape from him on the ground, but maybe we can do it in the air?"

She turned to Jack Frost.

"I'm not sure you can fly at all," she said.

"Of course I can!" Jack Frost roared. "I'll show you!"

He lurched into the air, wobbled sideways and bumped into a goblin, who fell into a holly bush with a squeal.

"I ... er ... meant to do that," said Jack Frost. "I'm a brilliant flyer."

The fairies rose into the air and
fluttered around him, flying first one way
and then another. He kept turning to
watch them, and his arms and legs flailed
as he got more and more dizzy.

The goblins were flying closer to watch
Jack Frost, and the fairies slowly led them

all to an open, grassy space. As Jack Frost
was glaring at Samira,
Rachel darted up
behind him and
unclipped the
cape. Then
she tossed it to
Samira, who
caught it and
hugged it to
her.

"Well done,
Rachel," she said.

"No!" wailed
Jack Frost.

*THUMP! THUMP! THUMP!* The
goblins fell on the frosty grass, and the Ice
Lord landed on top of them in a tangle of
arms, legs and enormous feet.

"You'll never get your other things back!" Jack Frost yelled.

"Let's leave before he gets back on his feet," said Kirsty.

"Good thinking," said Samira. "We have to return the cape to its hiding place and make a plan to get my other things back."

"We won't leave your side until everything is back where it belongs, and superheroes can start to protect people again," said Rachel.

"You are true friends," said Samira. "To the Silver Skyscraper – let's go!"

# The All-Seeing
# Eye Mask

# Contents

# Comics in Chaos

As soon as they were back in the Silver
Skyscraper, Samira dashed into her secret
room and put the cape back on the first
pedestal.

"It's good to see it back where it
belongs," she said.

Then she tapped her wand on the wall,

and it shimmered like the surface of a glassy pool.

"It reminds me of the Seeing Pool at the Fairyland Castle," said Kirsty.

Samira smiled.

"That's clever of you," she said. "That's exactly what it is."

A face appeared on the wall. It was blurry at first. Then it came into focus, and the three fairies saw that it was Queen Titania. They curtseyed, and Queen Titania smiled at them.

"Your Majesty, I am happy to report that we have the crimson cape back," said Samira.

"Well done, all of you," said the queen. "Rachel and Kirsty, I'm speaking to you through the Seeing Pool. Thank you for being here to help Samira. You are

proving your friendship once again. May
I ask you to stay a little longer? Will you
help Samira find her other two objects?"

"They have already promised me that
they will," said Samira.

The queen smiled again, and her kind
eyes sparkled.

"Good luck, all of you," she said.

Her image faded into mist, and the
wall returned to normal. Samira turned
to face Rachel and Kirsty.

"I'm going to use my super sight to
watch from the roof," she said. "I have to
find a clue somewhere in Fairyland that
will tell us what Jack Frost has done with
my other magical objects."

"Would you like us to come with you?" Rachel asked.

"Thank you, but it would be better for you to get some rest," said Samira. "I will come back and let you know as soon as there is any news."

Samira closed her secret room and then flew across to one of the window walls. She pushed her way out through the magical glass and waved to Rachel and Kirsty from the other side. Then she zoomed upwards and

out of sight.

Rachel and Kirsty looked at each other, thinking exactly the same thing. There was a pile of comic books on the coffee table and they couldn't wait to read them.

"Race you to the couch," said Rachel. "Ready, steady, go!"

They jumped on to the black couch

in glee, and picked up a comic book each. Leaning against the cushions, they opened their books and started to read.

"Which one have you chosen?" Kirsty asked after a little while.

"I've got *Catgirl and the Mountain of Mist*," said Rachel. "What about you?"

"*Spiderella and the Crystal Caves*," said Kirsty, frowning as she turned the pages. "But something's weird. Some friends have got trapped

in the caves, but Jill Jones has forgotten that she's Spiderella, and she hasn't saved them."

"This comic's a bit strange too," said Rachel. "Catgirl doesn't know that she has to help people in the High Mountains. She can't seem to tell who

needs her help."

Kirsty picked up another comic and flicked through it. Halfway through, the pages turned blank.

"These stories are boring," she said. The superheroes don't know what to do, so they're missing all the exciting things. Nothing's happening, and no one is helping the people who are in trouble."

"Something's wrong," said Rachel. "Let's take these comic books and show Samira. Maybe she'll know what to do."

# Rubble Trouble

Holding their comic books, the girls
hurried to the window and pressed
against the magical glass. Just like before,
they moved through it as if they were
pushing their hands into a rippling
pool. As soon as they were out, they
flew to the top of the spire. Samira was
standing on the platform at the top of

the spire, staring into the distance and turning slowly on the spot. Fluffy white clouds drifted past as Rachel and Kirsty fluttered up to join her.

"Have you seen anything that might help us?" Rachel asked.

Samira shook her head and sighed.

"We've found something strange," said Kirsty.

The girls showed Samira the stories in their comic books.

"Vicious villains!" Samira exclaimed. "These comics have all changed – I don't remember them being like this."

"It's as if what makes the superheroes super has just gone from the stories," said Rachel.

"It's because my all-seeing eye mask is missing," said Samira. "It helps superheroes to see where and who needs their help, and to know where to go and when. Your favourite superheroes don't even know that they are needed and—"

She held up her hand
suddenly, and put her head
on one side.

"What is it?" asked
Kirsty.

"There's a
problem in Goblin
Grotto," said
Samira.

The girls
were amazed,
and Samira smiled when she saw their
surprise.

"I have super hearing," she explained.
"There was a loud rumbling noise, and
then lots of goblins started yelling. Come
on – we have to investigate!"

The three fairies zoomed into the sky
and headed towards the goblin village,

flying in a triangle shape with Samira at
the front, her left arm outstretched.

"I hope that we're doing the right
thing," said Kirsty to Rachel as they flew
along. "Goblins don't always want help
from the fairies."

Soon they were flying over the familiar
wonky roofs of Goblin Grotto. Rachel

and Kirsty had visited the village several times, and they recognised the streets filled with ramshackle wooden huts where the goblins lived, and the big central square at the heart of the village.

Samira led them to where a crowd of goblins had gathered in one of the main streets. They were standing around a pile of rubble, pointing and shouting.

"Maybe we should go down in disguise," said Kirsty.

"There's no time," said Samira. "Someone's in trouble."

She whooshed down and landed on top of the rubble. Rachel and Kirsty were close behind her.

"What's happened here?" Samira asked.

The goblins were so worried that they

didn't even insult the fairies.

"The ground started shaking," one of them cried out. "One of the huts fell down and trapped a goblin. He's still under there."

"Tell him to push his way out," one goblin shouted.

"No, tell him to dig down until he comes out on the other side," yelled another.

"The other side of what, you nincompoop?" said a third goblin.

More and more goblins started shouting. Samira shook her head and bent down. She started to lift the rubble a piece at a time. Rachel and Kirsty bent down to help, but they couldn't lift a single piece of the rubble.

"It's so heavy," said Rachel, panting.

"Leave it to me," said Samira. "I have super strength – the goblin will soon be free."

The goblins in the crowd fell silent when they saw what Samira was doing. For a few moments the only sound was the crash of rubble as the Superhero Fairy moved it aside. Then there was a muffled squawk.

"About time!"

A dusty, grumpy-faced goblin
clambered out of the rubble and stuck his
tongue out at the fairies.

"He's free," said Kirsty with a sigh of
relief.

Suddenly a goblin in a black top hat
caught her eye. He was standing at
the front of a crowd of goblins, and he

was leaning back with his hand to his forehead.

"He looks more relieved than the goblin you saved," said Kirsty to Samira.

The goblin suddenly turned as if he had heard something. Then, with a look of utter panic, he raced away from the rubble.

"Oh my wings and wishes, someone needs help!" said Samira. "I can hear them shouting. Let's go."

She zoomed off, with Rachel and Kirsty close behind her.

# Strange Sculpture

Samira flew straight to the central square,
in the middle of the goblin village. When
they were still some distance away, they
saw a goblin standing on the roof of one
of the huts. He had his arms outstretched
as if he was trying to balance, and he
was wailing at the top of his voice.

"Get me
down! Let
me go!"

There was
a sudden
gust of
wind, and
the goblin
wobbled.
Then, with
a loud
squawk, he
slipped and
tumbled
downwards.

Samira moved so fast that she was just
a blur of purple and gold. In less than a
second, the goblin was safe in her arms.
She flew down to the ground and set him

on his feet. Goblins ran towards them,
squawking and babbling.

"What were you doing climbing on the
roof?"

"You dribbling idiot!"

"I didn't climb up there!" the goblin
wailed. "One minute I was eating a
green banana in my armchair, and the
next minute I was balancing on top of a
slippery roof. Ooh, my legs feel like jelly."

"I don't like all these accidents," an older goblin grumbled. "Someone needs to tell Jack Frost that his spells have side-effects. Ever since he started experimenting with  superhero spells, we can't leave our huts without pianos falling on our heads."

"And Frostman isn't always around to save us," said another goblin. "He takes very long lunch breaks."

"It sounds as if Jack Frost is making

emergencies happen," said Rachel, joining Samira.

"Yes, emergencies that need a superhero," said Kirsty, gazing around at the goblins. "Hey, look at that goblin over there – the one in the top hat. I've seen him before.  He was there when you saved the goblin from the rubble."

"He looks worried," said Samira.

As they watched, the goblin turned his

head sharply, as if he had heard something.

"He did that last time," said Kirsty.

"I remember," said Samira. "It was just before I heard the falling goblin call for help. Twinkling tiaras! Do you think he might have my all-seeing eye mask?"

"What makes you think that?" Rachel asked her.

"He seems to be able to sense where and when trouble is going to happen, and who needs help," said Samira. "That's a super-power that no goblin should have, but the all-seeing mask would give it to him. Look, he's moving away. Let's follow him."

The goblin set off along the path that led towards Jack Frost's castle. They could see it in the distance, sparkling with icicles. The goblin scurried along with his head down, and the fairies followed at a safe distance. They didn't want him to see them. The path sloped upwards, winding

around jagged rocks. The fairies lost sight of the goblin as he zigzagged around a huge rock.

"Let's catch up with him," said Samira. "I want to ask him if he knows anything about my magical objects."

They sped around the rock and skidded to a halt as they almost flew into the goblin in the top hat. He was standing next to a perfect ice sculpture of a goblin. Together, the fairies landed beside the sculpture and stared at it in amazement.

"This is the most detailed sculpture I've ever seen," said Samira.

"It even has tiny warts on its fingers," said Kirsty.

"Who made this?" Rachel asked.

The goblin in the top hat looked at her and gulped.

"No one made it," he said. "It's not a sculpture at all. It's a real goblin."

# Defrosted!

The fairies looked at the ice goblin
again, and shivered. No wonder the
goblin seemed scared.

"The poor thing looks surprised," said
Kirsty. "What happened to him?"

"He annoyed Jack Frost," said the
goblin in the top hat. "So Jack Frost
turned him to ice and then stomped back
to his castle."

"Jack Frost should learn to control his temper," said Samira. "But my super-breath can save this goblin."

She breathed on the ice goblin. Her warm breath sparkled as if it was made of fairy dust, and at once the ice began to turn from blue to green. A few seconds later, the ice goblin was real again. He was dripping wet, shivering and scowling at the fairies.

"This day is getting worse and worse," he squawked. "First Jack Frost yells at me, then I get freezing cold, and now I've got three fluff-brained fairies staring at me. Leave me alone."

He ran off, and the goblin in the top hat turned to follow him. Rachel and Kirsty zoomed over his head and landed in front of him, their hands on their hips.

"Hold on," said Kirsty.

"We want to ask you some questions."

"Like what?" the goblin snapped.

"Like how do you know where to go
when someone needs help?" said Rachel.

The goblin's
eyes opened
wide and he
took a step back.

"I just ... er ...
know," he said.

Samira was
standing behind
him.

"Did it all start
when Jack Frost

gave you something?" she asked.

The goblin jumped and spun around.

"Not telling," he said.

"Where are you hiding the all-seeing
eye mask?" asked Kirsty.

The goblin gave a frightened little yelp.

He glanced around as if someone might be listening.

"I'm not telling you anything," he hissed. "Jack Frost is always nearby."

"He can't hear you when he's in the Ice Castle," said Rachel.

"Besides, we can help you," Kirsty added.

The goblin just shook his head and pressed his lips together. Samira put her hand on his shoulder.

"I understand," she said in a gentle voice. "I know how scary

it feels to suddenly get these powers."

The goblin nodded, looking a little less stubborn.

"It makes it even harder because you can't do anything to help the goblins who are in trouble," Samira went on. "After all, you're not a superhero. It's not your job. Jack Frost has made you able to hear cries for help, without being able to do anything to save your friends."

"When you put it like that, it doesn't sound very fair," said the goblin. "But Jack Frost will be angry with me. I don't like him when he's angry."

"Samira can help," said Rachel.

"How?" the goblin asked, looking suspicious.

"All you have to do is give me the eye mask that Jack Frost asked you to hide," said Samira. "You see, as soon as it is in

my hands again, storybook superheroes
will be able to do their jobs. They just
need their powers back."

She held out her hand, and Rachel and

Kirsty hardly dared to breathe.

"Jack Frost is sure to find out if I give
you the eye mask," said the goblin.

"But you won't have to listen to all those cries for help any more," said Kirsty.

She and Rachel linked their little fingers, wishing as hard as they could for the goblin to make the right choice. Could he be brave enough to disobey Jack Frost?

# Hope in a Hat

The goblin's shoulders drooped as if he was giving in. But just at that moment, there was a crack of lightning and a rumble of thunder. The goblin jumped as if he had been stung.

"Jack Frost is coming," he exclaimed. "He's sure to find out what I've done.

Leave me alone!"

He dodged past Rachel and Kirsty and ran down the slope towards Goblin Grotto.

"We must stop him," Rachel cried out. "Samira, try again. I'm sure you almost changed his mind just then."

Samira zoomed upwards and flew over the goblin, landing in front of him with one knee bent and one hand flat on the

ground. Rachel and Kirsty landed beside the goblin.

"As long as you have the eye mask, you will be able to sense trouble and danger, but you won't be able to do anything about it," Samira said to him. "Your life will never be peaceful. I can make everything better. I can make your life go back to normal again. All you have to do is give back what belongs to me."

The goblin looked around at the jagged rocks. He gazed up at the grey Ice Castle.

"I think he's looking for Jack Frost," Rachel whispered to her best friend.

"Do the right thing, goblin," Kirsty urged under her breath.

The girls both crossed their fingers, and there was a long pause. The goblin shuffled his feet.

"Jack Frost doesn't have to know that you gave it to me," said Samira. "We could make it look as if I took it."

The goblin narrowed his eyes and glared at Samira.

"Leave me alone!" he shouted again, in a loud voice. "You will never make me betray Jack Frost!"

He flung his top hat at her with all his strength, and she dodged out of its way. The goblin blew a loud raspberry at her and then turned and ran away.

"Oh no," said Kirsty.

Samira sank to the ground as if her
legs were made of cotton wool. Kirsty
crouched down
beside her and
gave her a
hug.

"There has
to be a way
to change his
mind," Kirsty
said. "We won't
give up."

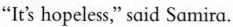

"It's hopeless," said Samira.

"Don't give up, Samira," said Rachel.
"I've got an idea."

She dashed over to the black top hat,
which now looked rather battered, and
picked it up.

"What is it?" asked Kirsty.

"Maybe the goblin was too scared to say how he really felt," she said. "Sometimes people are too frightened to admit when they need help. But don't you think it was strange that he threw his hat away? It looks like a special one."

Kirsty and Samira sat up straight, suddenly understanding Rachel's idea. Rachel looked into the top hat, and then a smile spread over her face. She reached inside the hat and pulled out a golden mask, glittering with magical sparkles.

"Speckled sprites, it's the all-seeing eye mask!" cried Samira.

She scrambled to her feet and Rachel handed her the eye mask. Samira hugged it to her chest, with happy tears shining in her eyes.

"I can't believe it," she said. "I can't wait to put it back where it belongs."

"Let's hurry back to the Silver Skyscraper and return it straight away," said Kirsty, glancing up at the Ice Castle. "Something tells me that we don't want to be here when Jack Frost finds out it's gone."

Side by side, the fairies rose into the sky.

"Now there is only one more magical object to get back," said Rachel. "I hope we can find it."

"I know we will," said Samira. "With you two by my side, I will never lose hope again!"

# The Lively
# Lasso

# Contents

# Fear and Fireworks

As the three fairies zoomed back to the Silver Skyscraper, the sky was a swirl of colour.

"Sunset in Fairyland is one of the most beautiful things I have ever seen," said Kirsty, swooping through shades of orange, lilac, yellow, pink and red.

The sun slipped behind a hill dotted with toadstool houses, and the sky turned to violet and then to dark blue. Soon it was sprinkled with tiny stars. When the fairies reached the Silver  Skyscraper, it was glowing in the light of the fairy moon. They flew to the platform and took the entry pod into Samira's apartment.

"There," said Samira, putting the all-seeing eye mask on a pedestal in her secret room. "Two out of three of my magical objects are back where they belong. I'm starting to feel as if things will soon be back to normal."

While Samira was closing her secret room, Rachel edged closer to Kirsty and whispered in her ear.

"I'm glad that Samira sounds full of hope again," she said. "I wish I could feel like that too. Suddenly I can't help worrying that we'll never find the lively lasso. How can we be of any use?"

"I don't know," said Kirsty in a low voice.

"I'm shaking just thinking about having to face Jack Frost. Maybe it would be better if Samira sent us home."

They hugged each other, feeling upset. Samira glanced at them and saw at once that something was wrong.

"What's the matter?" she asked, putting her arms around their shoulders.

"We're worried that we won't be able to find the lively lasso," said Rachel.

"We're no help."

"We're just useless," said Kirsty with a sigh.

"Of course you're not useless," said Samira in astonishment. "You've helped Fairyland more times than I can count."

"That was in the past," said Rachel. "We can't do it any more."

Samira frowned, looking confused. But before she could speak again, there was a bright burst of colour in the sky.

"FIREWORKS!" shouted the three fairies, forgetting their worries.

They rushed to the window and gazed into the distance. Someone somewhere was having a celebration. Rockets, fountains and star shells were exploding in the sky.

"I love fireworks," said Kirsty.

"Then let's go and see them," said Samira. "Maybe you two just need a break from chasing after Jack Frost and his goblins."

Eagerly, Rachel and Kirsty followed Samira through the glass window and out into the night air.

"It looks as if the display is on the seashore," said Samira.

They flew towards the ocean and hovered over the beach, but they couldn't see any other fairies.

"Perhaps the display has finished," said Rachel. "Maybe we're too late."

*BANG! POP! WHEEEEEE!* A volley of fireworks exploded above their heads. Rachel and Kirsty screamed and clung to each other.

"I can't stop trembling," said Rachel.

"Neither can I," said Kirsty. "And my teeth are chattering. What's wrong with us? We love fireworks."

"You look terrified," said Samira in surprise. "I don't understand – you are usually so brave. You're practically superheroes ... oh, of course! Rocketing rainbows!"

"What is it?" asked Rachel, squealing as another firework went off.

"Every fairy knows who you two are," said Samira. "Every fairy knows that Rachel Walker and Kirsty Tate will help her if she's in trouble. You're superheroes here in Fairyland."

"It's very kind of you to say so," said Kirsty. "But why would that make us afraid of fireworks?"

"My lively lasso helps superheroes to be confident and brave," Samira went on. "Without it, superheroes everywhere have lost their courage – and now that includes you!"

# Moonlight Mystery

"What are we going to do?" asked Rachel. "How can we help you if our courage is being drained away from us?"

"We just can't let Jack Frost take it," said Kirsty. "We have to hold on to all the bravery we have left, and find the lasso before it's too late."

*WHOOOSH! POP-POP! BANG!*

Another volley of fireworks lit up the sky.

"It's very strange that no one's here to watch these fireworks," said Rachel.

"My super-senses are starting to tingle," said Samira. "Something's wrong. Who would put on an amazing fireworks display and forget to invite an audience? Oh, my boots and bracelets, I think this could be a trap."

"Oh my goodness, let's get out of here!" said Rachel.

"I don't like traps," said Kirsty.

They started to fly away, but Samira

grabbed their hands and stopped them.

"Wait," she said. "Don't you see? The brave thing would be to keep going, knowing that it's a trap. I'm sure Jack Frost is behind this, which means that my lively lasso might be somewhere nearby. We have to try to find it."

Rachel and Kirsty squeezed each other's hand very tightly.

"We mustn't let Jack Frost scare us off," said Rachel.

"We'll come, even though we're scared," Kirsty added.

"That is a true superhero attitude," said Samira, smiling. "Now, let's try to work out where the fireworks are coming from."

Still hovering above the beach, they turned slowly, looking for the source of the fireworks. Then Kirsty saw a flash of light on the side of a white cliff.

"There!" she cried. "I think there must be a ledge on the side of that cliff. The

fireworks are coming from the middle of the cliff."

"Let's investigate," said Samira.

The fairies flew along beside the cliff, checking every ledge they saw. There was no one in sight, and no sign that any fireworks had been set off. Then Rachel gasped and pointed to a huge, dark hole in the cliff. It looked like a yawning mouth.

The fairies landed at the entrance and peered into the darkness.

"I can't see anything," said Kirsty.

Samira sniffed
the air.

"I can smell
fireworks," she
said. "I'm sure
they came from
in here. Let's go in
and explore."

"I was afraid she
was going to say

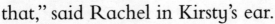

that," said Rachel in Kirsty's ear.

"I feel scared too," said Kirsty. "But
remember, it's only because the lively
lasso is missing. We have to pretend to be
brave."

"You're right," said Rachel. "We can't
let Samira go in there by herself."

Slowly, they tiptoed into the cave. They
could hear the drip-drip-drip of water.

It made a spooky, echoing sound. For
the first few steps, the moon lit their way.
But inky darkness stretched out ahead of
them.

"Don't worry, I've got my wand," said
Samira.

She lifted it up and gave it a little flick.
Dozens of tiny golden
sparks flew
from the tip
and floated
upwards,
lighting the way
ahead like
fireflies.

"Let's walk,"
said Rachel.
"I'm too
nervous to fly."

With Samira in the lead, they slowly made their way deeper and deeper into the cave.

"I've been thinking," said Kirsty. "I wonder why Jack Frost took your magical objects in the first place, Samira."

"Jack Frost steals when he wants something," said Samira. "I suppose he wanted to be a superhero."

"Yes, and he's calling himself 'Frostman'," said Rachel. "But now he's lost the mask and the cape, surely he can't be a proper superhero? Why does he still want the lasso?"

"Because it gives him confidence and bravery," said Samira. "As long as he has the lively lasso, Frostman will see himself as the perfect superhero. Leaping lizards, what's that?"

# Super Scary

Samira stopped suddenly, and Rachel and Kirsty bumped into her. Shivering with fear, they looked over her shoulders and saw a faint green light glowing up ahead. Then they heard a noise. *CREEEAAK! CREEAAK!* Rachel and Kirsty clung to each other, shaking.

"It's n-not r-really s-scary," Rachel reminded Kirsty. "We're only afraid b-because the l-lasso is m-missing."

"There's no reason to be scared," Kirsty agreed in a squeaky voice.

They followed Samira as she tiptoed forwards. The cave opened out into a vast, round chamber, with green lanterns placed on the rocks all around. In the

green glow, they could see that a giant-sized birdcage was dangling from the roof of the cave. A goblin was sitting inside it, cross-legged. He was resting his pointy chin in his hands, and he looked grumpy and fed up. When he saw the fairies, his scowl got even worse.

"Fairies," he groaned. "I thought you were going to be Jack Frost – I mean, Frostman. I've been waiting to be rescued for ages."

"I can have you out of there in a flash," said Samira, raising her wand.

"No!" the goblin shrieked, waving his hands at her. "Stop! Don't you dare rescue me."

"You don't really want to be stuck in a
cage, do you?"
said Kirsty. "I
wouldn't like it
one bit. Being
trapped is
scary."

"What I want
is my bed in
Goblin Grotto,"
the goblin complained. "But Jack Frost
– I mean, Frostman – has been trying to
be a superhero ever since he took your
magic objects, and now he needs to
practise being brave and heroic. He'll go
bananas if I'm not here to be rescued."

The fairies exchanged worried glances.

"We can't just leave him dangling in
the cage," said Rachel. "Even if he wants

to be here. It's hard to know what to do. I feel confused."

Suddenly a noise echoed around the cave. *WHOOOSH!*

"What is it?" cried Kirsty. "Another firework? I'm scared!"

"Get back!" cried Samira. "Into the shadows."

A blue bolt of lightning zoomed around the room, with Frostman standing on top of it. He stopped in front of the goblin, his hands on his hips. His spiky hair was slicked back. He was wearing a shiny electric blue jumpsuit with a little shoulder cape, and a blue eye mask with a white lightning bolt across it. A golden lasso was draped over his shoulder.

"Purple pumpkins!" said Samira. "That's my lively lasso!"

Frostman jumped down from the
lightning bolt and strode around the
chamber, gazing up at the goblin.

"Don't be afraid, cowering little
goblin," he said in a deep, booming voice.
"Frostman is here to save you!"

"About time," the goblin muttered.

Frostman tapped his wand on the cage,
and the door sprang open. The goblin
jumped out next to his rescuer.

"I can hardly believe what a fantastic superhero I am," said Frostman, stroking his beard. "In fact, I am the best superhero that ever was or ever will be."

He turned to gaze around the cave, and saw the fairies. His smug smile grew bigger and he waggled his bony fingers.

"I hoped my fireworks might bring a few nosy fairies here," he said. "At last I will have the chance to get my own back on you prissy pests."

Rachel and Kirsty shrank back, but then they saw Samira step forward to face Frostman with her head held high.

"I vow by Queen Titania's crown that I will stop you," she announced.

The best friends looked at each other.

"We can't let her do this alone," said Rachel.

"You're right," said Kirsty. "Even though it's scary, we have to stand beside her."

They stepped forward too, standing
on either side of the Superhero Fairy.
Frostman smirked at them.

"Fools," he said. "It's frosty time!"

# Trapped!

Frostman pointed his wand at the fairies and a rope of crackling blue electricity zapped out of the tip. It wrapped around them and knocked Samira's wand out of her hand. Then all three of them were lifted high into the air and flung into the cage. The door slammed shut and locked.

"Let us out!" Samira demanded,

shaking the bars of the cage.

Frostman threw back his head and cackled with laughter. Then he jumped on to the lightning bolt, pulling the goblin up with him.

"Farewell, foolish fairies!" he exclaimed. "No one will ever find you here. Ha!"

*WHOOOSH!* The lightning bolt shot out of the cave, and the fairies were left in the dangling cage, swinging gently to and fro in the green glowing light.

"Oh no!" cried Rachel, sinking to the floor of the cage.

"My wand!" Samira said with a groan.

Kirsty was trembling, but she had an idea. Even though she felt scared, she shouted at the top of her voice.

"Help! Help! Frostman, help!"

Rachel and Samira stared at her in astonishment. For a moment, the only noise was the faint *drip-drip-drip*

of water. Then there was a whooshing sound that grew louder and louder, and Frostman zoomed back into the chamber.

"Why am I back here?" he demanded, frowning. "I should be in the Ice Castle, being waited on by grovelling goblins."

"But you're a superhero now," said
Kirsty. "It looks as if the lively lasso is
making sure you act like one."

"We're trapped in here and we need
help," said Rachel. "Please get us out of
this cage."

Frostman
looked furious,
but he pointed
his wand at the
cage and the
door clicked
open. At once,
the fairies flew
out and Samira
picked up her
wand from the
floor. Rachel

and Kirsty landed beside her.

"What now?" she asked in a quiet voice.

"I've got an idea," said Kirsty. "Oh dear, my knees are knocking together."

"I'm here," said Rachel, holding her hand. "You're not on your own."

Kirsty took a deep breath and stepped forward to face Frostman.

"Do you really want to be a

superhero?" she asked. "With all your heart?"

"Yes," said Frostman. "Anyway, I'm already a superhero. Look at how super I am! Look at my super clothes and my super, super hair. Frostbitten fingers, I'm absolutely splendid!"

"Being a superhero isn't about your hairstyle or the clothes you wear," said Kirsty. "It's about how you behave, and how you treat other people."

Frostman folded his arms across his chest.

"Hairstyles and clothes sound like more fun," he muttered. "Sinister spellbooks, a superhero should be allowed to do whatever he wants."

"A true superhero would give Samira her lasso," said Kirsty. "After all, stealing things makes you a super villain, not a superhero."

"You don't understand," said Frostman. "You see, I really, really WANT this lasso."

"A true superhero always puts other people first," said Kirsty.

"A real superhero doesn't care about what he wants," Rachel added. "He always does the right thing for other people, no matter what."

They could see that Frostman was struggling. Part of him wanted to act like Jack Frost, but the lively lasso was telling the other part of him to do the right thing.

"At this very moment, all the

superheroes in the human world are in trouble," said Samira. "They're depending on you, Frostman. They need you to give the lively lasso back to me. It is the brave and right thing to do."

# Super Secrets

Rachel and Kirsty crossed their fingers. For a moment, no one moved. Then Frostman pulled the lasso off his shoulder and threw it at Samira's feet.

"I don't want to be a superhero anyway!" he roared. "It's turning me into a goody two shoes. To the Ice Castle!"

He stamped his foot, and there was a blinding flash of blue lightning. Frostman and the goblin disappeared.

Samira bent down and picked up the lively lasso. At once, Rachel and Kirsty felt their courage flowing through them again. It was like being warmed up from the inside.

Samira smiled at them.

"I can see that you're feeling better already," she said. "Superheroes everywhere will be themselves again, thanks to you."

She waved her wand in a circle, and a

warm breeze blew around the three of
them. It lifted them gently into the air
and transported them from the cave to
Samira's apartment in the blink of an
eye.

Samira flew to the portrait of the king
and queen, and pressed the ruby ring on
the queen's finger. At once, the whole
wall swivelled around and the fairies
fluttered into Samira's secret room.

"Now everything is as it should be," said Samira, placing the lively lasso on the third pedestal. "My three magical objects are back where they belong, and superheroes everywhere are under my protection again."

She turned to Rachel and Kirsty, and hugged them.

"You have both been truly heroic," she said. "Crimson crowns, I don't know how

you were brave enough to face Frostman
without the power
of the lively
lasso. None
of the
other
superheroes
has such
strength."

"We were
lucky," said
Rachel,
taking Kirsty's
hand and smiling. "We had each other."

"I will never forget your courage or
your kindness," said Samira.

"It has been an epic adventure,"
said Kirsty, gazing around at Samira's
apartment. "And it's been wonderful to

make a new fairy friend."

Smiling, Samira raised her wand. At
once, Rachel and Kirsty were dazzled
by a flurry of gold and purple stars.
When the stars cleared, the girls were
human again. They were back in their
seats in Tippington Cinema. On the
screen, Dragon Girl zoomed out of The
Mole's underground lair and into the sky.
Everyone in the cinema cheered.

"Yes!" Rachel called out.

"Go, Dragon Girl!" Kirsty exclaimed.

"Thank goodness for that," said the boy in the row in front. "For a minute I thought Dragon Girl had lost her powers for ever."

Rachel and Kirsty smiled at each other, thinking of their amazing secret. No time had passed in the human world, but all their adventures with Samira had returned the film to normal.

At last Tigerella and Dragon Girl thwarted The Mole's villainous plans and saved the world. As the credits rolled, Rachel and Kirsty stood up and collected their empty popcorn boxes.

"That was such an exciting film," said Rachel. "What did you think was the best part?"

"I loved it when Tigerella did a back flip over The Mole and lifted the jewels

out of his hands before he knew what was going on," said Kirsty. "What about you?"

"My favourite part was the happy ending, when Tigerella and Dragon Girl went back to their secret identities," said Rachel.

"That makes two happy endings for us to celebrate," said Kirsty with a grin. "Shooting stars, this calls for an ice-cream!"

"I'll race you to the ice-cream shop," said Rachel, laughing. "KAPOW!"

Now it's time for Kirsty and
Rachel to help...

# Monica the
# Marshmallow Fairy

**Read on for a sneak peek...**

"Welcome back to Wetherbury!" said
Kirsty Tate.

Her best friend Rachel Walker placed
a raspberry-coloured suitcase on Kirsty's
bed.

"I'm so happy to be here with you for
the week," she said. "I'll just unpack my
things and then we can go and play."

As she reached out to open the suitcase,
Mrs Tate came in holding the phone.

"It's your Aunt Harri," she told Kirsty.

Kirsty took the phone and Mrs Tate left

the room. As Kirsty chatted to her aunt, a huge smile lit up her face, and Rachel hopped from foot to foot, longing to know what was being said. Aunt Harri worked at the Candy Land sweet factory outside the village, and Kirsty and Rachel thought that she might just have the best job in the world.

Kirsty hung up and clapped her hands together.

"Rachel, Aunt Harri's going to be here any minute," she said, brimming with excitement. "She's going to pick us up in the Candy Land van for a special trip."

Rachel squealed, and the girls linked hands and spun around in delight.

"Do you think she's going to take us to the Candy Land factory?" Kirsty said.

"If she does, I wonder if we'll see the Sweet Fairies again," said Rachel.

She and Kirsty shared a happy smile.
The last time they had seen Aunt Harri,
they had been caught up in a magical
adventure with their fairy friends.
Because they had promised to always
keep the secrets of Fairyland, they
couldn't tell anyone else about their
adventures. It was always wonderful to be
able to talk about magic together.

Just then, Rachel's raspberry-coloured
suitcase started to glow. The clasps rattled,
and then the suitcase burst open and a
tiny fairy fluttered out. She was wearing
a buttoned denim skirt, a fluffy jumper
and pink sandals, and her shiny brown
hair swished around her face.

"Hello, Rachel and Kirsty," she said.
"I'm Monica the Marshmallow Fairy."

"It's amazing to meet you," said Kirsty.
"Welcome to Wetherbury . . . but what

are you doing here?"

"I'm one of the Candy Land Fairies," said Monica, perching on the open lid of the suitcase. "I'm here to take you to the Sweet Factory in Fairyland. The Candy Land Fairies are hoping to speak to you – will you come?"

The girls exchanged a look of sheer delight. They had been to the Sweet Factory before, and they knew that it was a magical place full of sweet fairy treats.

Read **Monica the Marshmallow Fairy**
to find out what adventures are in store for Kirsty and Rachel!

**Calling all parents, carers and teachers!**
The Rainbow Magic fairies are here to help
your child enter the magical world of reading.
Whatever reading stage they are at, there's
a Rainbow Magic book for everyone!
Here is Lydia the Reading Fairy's guide to
supporting your child's journey at all levels.

## ① Starting Out

Our Rainbow Magic Beginner Readers are perfect for first-time readers who are just beginning to develop reading skills and confidence. Approved by teachers, they contain a full range of educational levelling, as well as lively full-colour illustrations.

## ② Developing Readers

Rainbow Magic Early Readers contain longer stories and wider vocabulary for building stamina and growing confidence. These are adaptations of our most popular Rainbow Magic stories, specially developed for younger readers in conjunction with an Early Years reading consultant, with full-colour illustrations.

## ③ Going Solo

The Rainbow Magic chapter books – a mixture of series and one-off specials – contain accessible writing to encourage your child to venture into reading independently. These highly collectible and much-loved magical stories inspire a love of reading to last a lifetime.

www.rainbowmagicbooks.co.uk

"Rainbow Magic got my daughter reading chapter books. Great sparkly covers, cute fairies and traditional stories full of magic that she found impossible to put down" – Mother of Edie (6 years)

"Florence LOVES the Rainbow Magic books. She really enjoys reading now" – Mother of Florence (6 years)

# The Rainbow Magic Reading Challenge

Well done, fairy friend – you have completed the book!
**This book was worth 10 points.**

See how far you have climbed on the
**Reading Rainbow** opposite.

The more books you read, the more points you will get,
and the closer you will be to becoming a Fairy Princess!

**Do you want your own Reading Rainbow?**
1. Cut out the coin below
2. Go to the Rainbow Magic website
3. Download and print out your poster
4. Add your coin and climb up the Reading Rainbow!

There's all this and lots more at
**www.rainbowmagicbooks.co.uk**

You'll find activities, competitions, stories, a special
newsletter and complete profiles of all the
Rainbow Magic fairies. Find a fairy with your name!